KLOOZ
Undercover
Goalie

by J. Banscherus
translated by Ann Berge
illustrated by Ralf Butschkow

STONE ARCH BOOKS
www.stonearchbooks.com

First published in the United States in 2009
by Stone Arch Books
151 Good Counsel Drive, P.O. Box 669
Mankato, Minnesota 56002
www.stonearchbooks.com

First published by Arena Books
Rottendorfer str. 16, D-97074
Würzburg, Germany

Library of Congress Cataloging-in-Publication Data
Banscherus, Jürgen.
    [Tore, Tricks und schräge Typen. English]
    Undercover Goalie / by J. Banscherus; illustrated by Ralf Butschkow.
    p. cm. — (Pathway Books. Klooz)
    Originally published: Tore, Tricks und schräge Typen. Germany:
Arena Verlag, 1996.
    ISBN 978-1-4342-1219-1 (library binding)
    [1. Mystery and detective stories.] I. Butschkow, Ralf, ill. II. Title.
PZ7.B22927Und 2009
[Fic]—dc22   2008031575

Summary: The goalie on the Horton Street Hornets is great during
practice, but he's terrible during real games. Klooz has been hired to
figure out what's making the goalie freeze up. Klooz hates sports, but this
case is putting him on the field. Will he solve the mystery — and help the
Hornets win?

Creative Director: Heather Kindseth
Graphic Designer: Kay Fraser

1 2 3 4 5 6 14 13 12 11 10 09

Printed in the United States of America

Table of contents

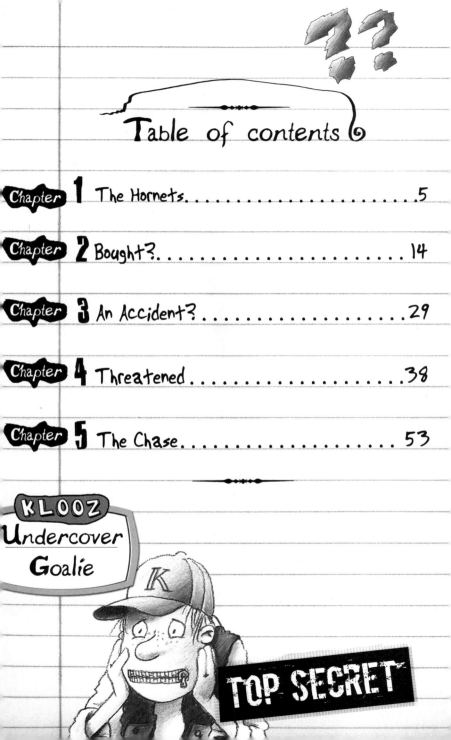

KLOOZ
Undercover
Goalie

TOP SECRET

CHAPTER 1

The Hornets

Until about two months ago, I thought soccer was about as interesting as long walks on Sunday afternoons or shopping with my mom. I would have thought you were crazy if you told me I would end up being a goalie.

Klooz, the private detective, play in a soccer match? Klooz, solver of the hardest cases, risk being embarrassed by the other team? No way. It sounded insane.

Then one day, Jana talked to me. She's the best soccer player at my school. Nobody can beat her.

We were at recess. I had a piece of my favorite Carpenter's chewing gum and a bottle of fresh milk.

I was trying to relax. We had just taken a math test. Math tests are not one of my favorite hobbies.

"Hey, Klooz!" called Jana.

"What?" I asked.

"The team needs your help," she said. "Right away!"

I pushed my gum from my left cheek to my right cheek and said, "I don't play soccer."

Jana shook her head. "That's not what this is about," she said. "We need you as a detective!"

As a detective? That was more like it.

For a few weeks, I hadn't gotten any new cases. Thank goodness I had something new to work on. A detective has to stay in training if he doesn't want his skills to get rusty.

"Okay, tell me about it," I said as casually as possible. I didn't want to show Jana how excited I was about having a new case.

Horton Street Hornets

Jana began to explain. "I play on a team in my neighborhood," she said. "The Horton Street Hornets. Right now there's a city-wide soccer tournament. Almost all the neighborhood teams are involved."

She paused for a moment. Then she went on, "We should definitely win it, because we honestly have the best players. But sometimes Oliver lets in easy goals. That's why we've lost the first two games. And if we aren't careful, we're going to be out of the tournament very soon."

"Slow down," I said. "First of all
is Oliver? And why is it so terrible if
sometimes he misses an easy goal?"

I learned that Oliver went to our school,
but he was in a different grade. Jana said
that at soccer practice he played like a
world champion, but during the games, he
played like he couldn't see.

"Something's not right with him," said Jana finally. "I've tried to watch Oliver to figure it out, but when you're busy playing, it's kind of difficult. Maybe you can figure out what's up, Klooz."

Like I said, I was really happy to get a new case. But what Jana had just told me sounded like no big deal. Oliver was probably just nervous to play in games in front of so many people.

"Soccer's not my thing," I said. "I'm sorry, Jana."

I didn't want to waste my time at the soccer field. There could be something much more interesting somewhere else. This wasn't a case for me.

"Please, Klooz!" Jana begged. "Do it for me!"

Then she put her hands on my
shoulders and bent down to look me in the
eye. She's a lot taller than I am.

Jana doesn't let go of things, like a
snake. Everyone knows that. Maybe that's
why she usually gets what she wants.

"All right, all right," I mumbled. "I'll come to one game. Then I'll decide if I want to take the case."

Then I told Jana about my payment. I always get five packs of my favorite chewing gum when I solve a case.

Jana thought about it for a while. She chewed on her fingernails. Finally, she shook my hand. "It's a deal," she said. "Just figure out what's up with Oliver."

We made a plan to meet after school at the soccer field near Jana's apartment. That's where the game was between Jana's team, the Horton Street Hornets, and the Tigers from Fulton Street.

Neither team had won a game yet in the tournament. Jana's team wanted to finally win one.

"Do your teammates know that I'm going to investigate?" I asked.

Jana shook her head. "They laughed at me when I said I was suspicious of Oliver," she said.

I had my doubts too, but I kept them to myself. Five packs of gum were riding on this game.

CHAPTER 2

Bought?

On my way home from school, I realized I didn't have any more gum. I found two dollars in my pocket. That was enough for two packs.

The after-school rush was in full swing at Olga's newspaper stand. As always, kids were buying candy, chips, and lots of other healthy things.

"Hello, Klooz," Olga greeted me. She wiped a bit of sweat from her forehead. "Would you like a glass of lemonade? I need one too."

Of course I couldn't say no.

"What's up with you?" she asked, as she placed two glasses on the counter.

"I haven't heard about any new cases lately," Olga added. "Have you thrown in the detective towel?"

I took a big drink. "Of course not," I said. "I may have a new case at the moment. But I'm pretty sure it's nothing."

"Nothing?" asked Olga curiously.

It didn't take long to explain everything about Jana, Oliver, and the Horton Street Hornets. It wasn't an important case. Why should I keep it a secret?

After I told her the story, Olga was quiet. She thought about it for a while.

"What if Oliver was bought?" she asked.

"What does that mean?" I asked.

"Maybe he is being paid to make sure his team loses," Olga said.

Man, that Olga is smart! I never would have thought of that!
"Thanks for the tip, Olga!"
I said.

I stood up to leave. A snack was waiting for me at home.

After I ate, my mom made me finish
my homework. Some people just don't
know that there are more important things
than math and spelling.

It wasn't far to the soccer field. The field
was really nothing more than a dirty gray
spot with high fences behind the goals.

It was clear to me right away that it was not the championship game of the tournament, because there weren't many fans there to watch. Only about a dozen kids had come to watch the match between the Horton Street Hornets and the Tigers from Fulton Street. Most of them stood on the sidelines.

Three boys, all a little bit older than me, had gathered behind Oliver's goal. I decided to pay extra attention to them.

As both teams warmed up, Jana came up to me. Her left knee was already bleeding, but she didn't seem to notice it.

"That is Oliver," she said. She pointed at a boy who had just blocked a goal. "Did you see how well he did that?" Jana asked. "Oliver is really good. He just plays so badly most of the time!"

Soon the game started. Jana was the
only girl, but she quickly showed the
others what she could do. She ran and
had great passes. She dribbled past the
opponents. She could always find an open
teammate to pass to. She scored three
goals for the Hornets.

By halftime, the score was 3–0, with the
Hornets winning. Jana came over to talk
to me.

"What did you think of Oliver, Klooz?"
she asked.

"He didn't have anything to do," I said. "You were just too good. But do you know who those guys are? The ones who have been standing behind the goal."

I pointed to the three boys who had been standing behind Oliver's goal. They had slowly wandered to the other side of the field.

"Of course I know them," answered Jana. "That's Kevin, Dennis, and Mark. They think they are the best!"

"Could they be paying Oliver to lose?"
I asked.

Jana laughed. "No way! Those three want to play for the Hornets!" she said.

In the second half, the game changed. All of a sudden, the Fulton Street Tigers were much better. Soon the game was tied.

As far as I could tell, all three goals were too hard for Oliver to stop. He wasn't cheating.

Just before the end of the game, the Tigers had a penalty kick.

The middle forward for the Tigers placed the ball on the field. He took a running start, faked out Oliver, and kicked.

The ball hit Oliver right in the foot. The ball bounced off the goal post and flew over the goal, out of bounds.

The excitement had barely died down before Jana faked out three Tigers to score another goal. That made the score 4 to 3. The final whistle sounded. The Hornets had won the game!

Oliver and Jana were buried under a pile of happy teammates and fans. Mark, Kevin, and Dennis, however, did not cheer. I watched as they disappeared, hands in their pockets and mad looks on their faces.

Why were they angry if they wanted to play for the Hornets? I couldn't figure it out.

Only one thing was sure: Oliver wasn't guilty. No one had paid him to lose.

After a while, Jana freed herself from her fans. She came over to talk to me.

"Congratulations, " I said.

"Thanks," she said. "You brought us luck, Klooz. Did you enjoy yourself?"

I shrugged my shoulders. "It's weird, all this running around," I said.

She laughed. "I like it," she said. "What do you think about Oliver?"

"I don't think he's guilty," I said. "Didn't you see the last save?"

"You're right, that was great!" Jana said. "He can't be guilty."

"Well, then there's no case for me to solve," I said.

"I guess not," Jana said. "I'll bring you the gum tomorrow."

I shook my head. "Forget the gum," I said. "I didn't have to do anything." Then I left.

I walked over to Olga's newspaper stand. Mark, Kevin, and Dennis were there, buying chewing gum. Of course, they weren't buying Carpenter's. Obviously, they didn't have good taste.

After they were gone, Olga leaned over the counter and asked, "Do you know them?" I nodded. "They were really complaining," she said. "Something about people named Jana and Oliver. Isn't the goalie on the Horton Street Walnuts named Oliver?"

"The Horton Street Hornets," I corrected her. "Yes. The goalie's name is Oliver. If he hadn't played so well today, the Hornets would have lost."

"Then Oliver isn't being bribed," Olga decided.

"No, he isn't," I replied, but I had a weird feeling in my stomach.

I couldn't fall asleep that night. I kept thinking about the soccer game. I kept seeing the angry faces of Kevin, Mark, and Dennis.

If they wanted to play for the Hornets, then why weren't they excited that the team had won? I was sure there was something fishy going on with those three boys.

At around midnight, I drank two bottles of milk to help me sleep.

CHAPTER 3

An Accident?

The next morning I was so tired I almost brushed my teeth with a comb and used my T-shirt as a towel.

Seven hours of sleep isn't enough for anyone, even a private detective.

On the way to school, I ran into Oliver. That woke me up.

His left eye was swollen and his lip was big. I could see bruises on his chin.

"What happened to you?" I asked.

He shrugged. "An accident," he answered.

I wanted to talk to Jana right away, but I couldn't find time during school. I really had to think about this case. I did my best thinking at home in bed, so after school, I hurried home.

When I got home, I put two pieces of gum in my mouth and poured myself a big glass of milk. Then I began to organize my thoughts.

Obviously, Oliver was trying to pull my leg. An accident? Yeah right! He would have had to tie a bear to his back to look like that.

No, his injury definitely had something to do with the match between the Horton Street Hornets and the Tigers from Fulton Street.

I went over the facts.

The Hornets had won the match. Oliver even blocked a penalty kick.

When I thought about it, it almost seemed like he had accidentally made the save. Had he actually wanted to let the ball through?

During both halves, Dennis, Kevin, and Mark were standing behind Oliver's goal. They didn't talk to him. Even though they wanted to play on the team, they were angry that the Hornets had won. And today Oliver's face looked like it had been run over by a steamroller.

I just knew something fishy was going on. Those three guys probably paid Oliver to lose the game. Then, when he blocked the penalty kick and broke their agreement, they beat him up.

I had to figure out right away why the three boys had bribed Oliver and why Oliver would let himself be bribed.

I decided one thing. The boys had probably scared Oliver, and three against one didn't look good for Oliver.

I called Jana and asked her to come over. She didn't live very far away. Just a few minutes later, I heard the doorbell ring.

I told her my new thoughts on Oliver and the three boys. She understood right away that I had decided to take up the case again. She didn't even mind when I mentioned my payment.

"What are you going to do?" she wanted to know.

I had a plan ready. "It doesn't make sense to talk to Oliver," I said. "He'll deny everything. You're going to have to put me in as goalie."

Jana was speechless for a moment. Then she rolled her eyes and said, "Gosh, that's a great idea! And my grandpa will play middle forward!"

"When is your next game?" I asked.

"In one week," answered Jana.

I thought about it. Then I said, "There's really not much time. But it has to work."

I explained my plan to Jana. She would coach me for the next few days. Soon, I'd be so good that no one would notice that Oliver was gone. Then we just had to wait for Dennis, Kevin, and Mark to come to me.

Jana agreed to the plan. I was going to be the goalie for the Horton Street Hornets.

I got my old tennis shoes out of the basement. Then I wrapped old scarves and rubber band around my knees as protection. I looked like a plucked chicken. I wished I'd never taken the stupid case.

Every day, Jana and I met at the soccer field to train for a few hours. On the first day, I couldn't make a single save. But after ten hours of training, I was good enough that Jana had to work hard to get a goal.

She said I was talented. I had no idea if she was right. All I knew was that I was so sore, I could barely get out of bed the next morning. But I couldn't give up the case.

The next match was against the undefeated Bombers from Main Street. The day before the match, Jana and I sat together at the field after we practiced. Sweat dripped down my back, and my hands were burning like fire.

I asked her, "Does Oliver know he's not playing tomorrow?"

Jana smiled. "We're lucky, Klooz," she replied. "Oliver has the flu."

"Do the others know I'm the replacement?" I asked.

"I told everybody. They're all okay with it. I told them that you're as good as Oliver. Do you think Dennis, Kevin, and Mark will take the bait?" she asked nervously.

I stood up. "You can count on it," I said. "Or my name isn't Klooz."

CHAPTER 4

Threatened

The three boys did take the bait. Right after Jana left, Kevin, Dennis and Mark appeared.

They waited until Jana turned the corner and then walked up to me. No one else was anywhere nearby.

"You're pretty good," Mark said.

"We've been watching you," said Dennis.

"No one will miss Oliver," Kevin added. "You are way better."

The three boys got closer. Suddenly Kevin and Mark grabbed my shoulders. Dennis stared directly into my eyes. I knew what was going to happen.

And it did. "You're not going to win tomorrow," Dennis said. His voice sounded friendly.

"Why not?" I asked.

"Because you'll be in big trouble if you do win," said Kevin.

Mark put me into a headlock. It was becoming rather uncomfortable.

"Why do you want the Hornets to lose?" I croaked.

"We have our reasons," replied Mark. He let me out of the headlock.

I was silent. I had to let them suffer a little bit. Then I said, "Fine. But it will cost you something. Twenty dollars!"

"You are crazy!" cried Kevin. "We're the ones making the demands. Lose the game, and everything is all right. Is that clear?"

"Remember what happened to Oliver," said Dennis. He grinned. Then the three boys turned and left.

So I had been right. The three boys threatened Oliver so that he'd lose. Oliver was frightened, but he didn't get any money for it.

Now, the three boys were trying their tricks on me. But that's where they went wrong. They were in for a surprise!

Deep in thought, I made my way back home. I was silent at dinner, too, even though my mom ordered pizza. Usually pizza makes me really happy. But not tonight.

"You're so quiet," said my mother. "Do you have a difficult case?"

"No, it's not hard," I said. "I actually solved it."

"That's great!" my mother said. "You should celebrate!"

I tried to smile. "Yeah," I said.

I wondered if I should tell my mom what was going to happen the next day.

She didn't really like hearing about my cases, especially when they were dangerous. It was probably better to keep my mouth shut.

On the other hand, I had to talk to someone. Dennis, Kevin, and Mark weren't playing around. They were serious about what they were going to do.

So I said, "Mom, I'm scared I'm going to get beat up tomorrow."

My mom started asking questions. She didn't stop until she knew all the details of the case.

Then she looked at me for a long time. I knew what she was going to say.

She'd say, "Tomorrow, you are not allowed to leave the house!" Then I'd have to stay home from school and I'd never solve the case.

But that isn't what she said. To my surprise, my mom asked, "How many players are on the Hornets?

"Including the substitute players, there are eleven or twelve people," I answered.

"Eleven or twelve people?" Mom repeated. She smiled. "Don't you think they could protect you from three boys?"

"Of course they could," I said.

My mom smiled. "Okay then," she said.

"But what if they run into me on the way to school or someplace?" I said. "Jana and the others can't always be there to help me!"

"You'll have to think of something," said my mother. "Are you a private detective or not?"

"So I'm allowed to play, Mom?" I asked.

"As long as you're careful, yes," she said. She gave me a kiss and added, "Right now, though, it's time for you to go to bed."

I didn't go to sleep right away. I thought for a while. After an hour, my plan was solid. If my plan worked, Kevin, Dennis, and Mark would finally leave me and the Hornets alone once and for all.

That night, I slept like a rock. All my fears went away.

On the way to school, I met Jana. I told her what had happened at the soccer field. Then I told her my plan. She said she'd do whatever it took to help me.

After school, I went to Olga's to tell her the plan. She said she'd help us. She even gave me a pack of gum for good luck. I was so nervous that I chewed the whole pack at once!

I arrived at the soccer field at 2 o'clock. The game was supposed to begin at 3.

At first, my teammates laughed about my kneepads made of old scarves. I had attached them to my knees with rubber bands again, so I guess they did look kind of funny.

Jana explained to the other kids that I was not only the substitute goalie, but also a detective. They all smiled.

I told them my plan. Except for the boy who had to go to flute practice right away after the game, the whole team wanted to help me with the plan. They seemed excited about it.

Then the Main Street Bombers arrived at the field.

My heart sank through my stomach into my shorts. They were each almost a head taller than we were! No wonder they'd never lost a game. I whispered to Jana that they really should be called the Main Street Skyscrapers.

She laughed. "I'm counting on you, Klooz!" she whispered. "You are at least as good as Oliver!"

Just before the game began, Mark, Kevin, and Dennis appeared. They stood behind the goal, just like they'd done with Oliver. I tried not to look at them, but I could feel them staring at me.

That day, I made amazing saves. I blocked shots that were high, low, to the left or right, or directly at me.

Somehow, I always knew where the ball
was going to fly. The Bombers from Main
Street started to worry.

At halftime, the score was 0–0. During the break, I stayed with the team. Kevin, Mark, and Dennis waved at me, trying to get me to come over and talk to them.

I acted like I didn't notice anything. With Jana and the others around, I felt completely safe.

In the second half of the game, the Bombers from Main Street put the pressure on. But they still couldn't score a goal.

At the end of the game, it was still tied 0–0. Of course, it would have been great to win, but a tie was almost as good. After all, the Bombers were one of the best teams in the city!

I was the hero of the day. But Kevin, Mark, and Dennis didn't think I was a hero.

"We did it," I said after my teammates stopped hugging me. "Now the plan begins. We'll meet at the park in fifteen minutes, okay?"

"Okay, Klooz!" my teammates said.

CHAPTER 5

The Chase

Then I ran. And ran. And ran. I could hear footsteps pounding behind me.

PARK

Kevin, Mark, and Dennis had seen me leave the field alone. They were chasing after me.

The chase took us through the city. My side started to hurt and I was breathing really fast. The other three looked like they were having problems too.

I got slower when we got closer to the park. The three boys started to gain on me. Soon, they had me. Gasping, they pushed me onto a bench.

So far, my plan had worked perfectly. Now it was time for the others to appear. Otherwise, I was going to get a beating. I really didn't feel like getting beat up.

"Wait!" I said. "I'm a detective!"

The three boys started laughing. They thought I was joking.

"You are, Klooz?" yelled Kevin. "Well, then we're the three kings!"

"Ha ha," I growled. "I really am a detective. Jana thought that Oliver lost the first two games on purpose. That's why she hired me."

Mark raised his fist. "That's enough!" he yelled.

Right then, Jana and the other Hornets leapt out of the bushes. The three boys didn't have a chance. Within seconds, my teammates were holding onto them. They couldn't run.

"Everything okay, Klooz?" asked Jana.

I nodded. "That was close," I said.

I still had one question for Kevin, Mark, and Dennis. "Why did you guys pressure me and Oliver?" I asked them.  "What's your problem with the Hornets?"

Kevin stared angrily at Jana. "We don't have any problem with the Hornets. We have a problem with her!" he said loudly.

"What do you mean?" I asked.

Mark said, "Since Jana's been on the Hornets, she decides everything. She decides who's allowed to be on the team, who the substitutes are, and where games are played. And no one does anything to stop her!"

"We wanted to be on the team," explained Dennis. "Jana wouldn't let us."

"We're at least as good as the others!" cried Mark.

"So when she wouldn't let us on the team, we decided that the Hornets would not win the tournament," Kevin said.

"That's because we knew a loss would be the worst thing that could happen to her," Dennis added. "If you hadn't shown up, Klooz, it would have worked!"

It was quiet for a moment.

Jana scratched her ear and stared at her cleats. She looked pretty upset. I couldn't tell if what the three boys had said was true or not.

Finally, I was the one who broke the silence.

"So what do we do?" I asked.

"Let's beat them up!" called one of the boys from the Hornets. He threw his arm around Kevin's neck.

"Stop!" I cried. "I do not like violence. I will not take part in it. I have a better idea. This is the only way to find out if you deserve to be on the Hornets or not. Could you give me your scarf, Jana?"

I tied the scarf around the lowest branch of a nearby tree. Then I measured off twelve paces and marked the place with a stone.

Tim   Pablo   Niko   Jacob   Eddy   Luca

One of the players had brought a soccer ball along with him. I asked if I could borrow it. He tossed me the ball, and to my surprise, I caught it.

"Everyone has one shot," I said to Kevin, Mark, and Dennis. "If any of you hit the scarf, you can join the Hornets."

"Have you gone crazy, Klooz?" Jana asked angrily.

I didn't pay attention to her. "Who agrees with my suggestion?" I asked. After a moment, everyone raised their hands — except Jana.

"See?" I said to her. She gave me an angry look.

Kevin looked at the scarf tied to the tree. "What if we don't hit it?" he asked.

I grinned. "Then you were kept off the team for a good reason, and you've been mean to Jana for no reason. If you miss, you go home in your underwear. Your clothes stay here. You can pick them up tomorrow morning at Olga's newspaper stand."

"You are a dirty rat, Klooz," mumbled Kevin. He stood up and got ready for his one shot.

As he walked up to the ball, we all held our breaths. Kevin shot, but he missed by a hair.

Dennis was the next to go. He didn't make it either.

Mark was nervous. His shot wasn't even close. The ball went flying off, deep into the woods.

So, a few minutes later, three boys in their underwear crept home through the forest. I made a neat pile of their clothes. I would bring it to Olga's newspaper stand the next morning.

Jana walked up and put five packs of gum into my hand. She was really happy about what had happened.

"Thanks a lot, Klooz," she said. "If we ever need a substitute goalie, you're our guy."

For a second, I wanted to ask why I couldn't be the main goalie. After all, I had saved the tie against the Main Street Bombers. But Jana was probably still a little mad at me.

So I put a piece of gum in my mouth and said, "Once is enough for me. Too much physical activity is terrible for my detective skills!"

That was the end of my career as goalie.

I was sore for days after the game. I decided that I'd never take on another case that had anything to do with sports.

I heard Oliver was glad about what happened to the three bullies. He never said anything to me, but he winked at me in school one day.

The Hornets went all the way to the city championship game. I went to watch the final game. The Hornets lost 0–4 against the Main Street Bombers, even though Oliver played a fantastic game. I like to think that if I'd been playing, they might have won.

I guess Kevin, Mark, and Dennis were probably glad to hear that the Hornets lost the championship. They're playing for the Fulton Street Tigers now, and they're looking forward to next year's tournament. I bet they can't wait to take on the Horton Street Hornets when the two teams meet.

Jana is on a new team now. It's called the Goats. There was actually a big article on her in the paper. Her teammates just voted her team captain.

The end

About the Author

Jürgen Banscherus is a worldwide phenomenon. There are almost a million Klooz books in print, and they have been translated into Spanish, Danish, Thai, Chinese, and eleven other languages. He has worked as a newspaper writer, a research scientist, and a teacher. His first book for children was published in 1985. He lives with his family in Germany.

About the Illustrator

Ralf Butschkow was born in Berlin. He works as a freelance graphic designer and illustrator, and has published more than 50 books for children. Critics have praised his work as "thoroughly enjoyable," "creatively original," and "highly recommended."

Glossary

accident (AK-si-duhnt)—something that took place unexpectedly, often involving someone getting hurt

bribed (BRIBED)—gave money to someone to get them to do something

career (kuh-REER)—the job a person has

champion (CHAM-pee-uhn)—winner

injury (IN-juh-ree)—damage or harm

neighborhood (NAY-bur-hud)—a small area or section where people live

opponents (uh-POH-nuhnts)—the people playing against your team

replacement (ri-PLAYSS-muhnt)—a person used in place of another

substitute (SUB-stuh-toot)—a person used in place of another

suspicious (suh-SPISH-uhss)—feeling like something is wrong or bad

threatened (THRET-uhnd)—frightened

tournament (TUR-nuh-muhnt)—a series of contests in which a number of people or teams try to win the championship

Discussion Questions

1. Why didn't Kevin, Mark, and Dennis like Jana? What would have been some better ways for them to handle their problem?

2. Oliver and Klooz were both threatened by Kevin, Mark, and Dennis. What are some ways to deal with bullies?

3. Klooz becomes the substitute goalie to work on his investigation. What other ways can you think of that he could have cracked the case?

Writing Prompts

1. At the beginning of this book, Klooz thinks that he doesn't like soccer. By the end of the book, he's a great soccer player. Write about a time when you tried something new and found out that you were good at it.

2. Olga and Klooz are friends even though Olga is older than Klooz. Write about a friend that you have who is older than you.

3. This book is a mystery story. Write your own mystery story!

More Klooz for

KLOOZ

The Big Stink

by J. Banscherus

KLOOZ

Computer Crook

by J. Banscherus

Need a detective?
Call on KLOOZ!

Mystery Fans!

KLOOZ
The Mysterious Mask

by J. Banscherus

STONE ARCH Mystery

KLOOZ
Trouble Under the Big Top

by J. Banscherus

STONE ARCH Mystery

This smart, funny kid has a good head on his shoulders and a good brain under that baseball cap he always wears. The whole town knows that **Klooz** is clever and cool, but his friends and family know something else: **Klooz** is loyal. He never lets you down.

Internet Sites

Do you want to know more about subjects related to this book? Or are you interested in learning about other topics? Then check out FactHound, a fun, easy way to find Internet sites.

Our investigative staff has already sniffed out great sites for you!

Here's how to use FactHound:

1. Visit *www.facthound.com*

2. Select your grade level.

3. To learn more about subjects related to this book, type in the book's ISBN number: **9781434212191**.

4. Click the **Fetch It** button.

FactHound will fetch the best Internet sites for you!